Hilltop Hospital

CW00926523

Happy Birthday, Dr Matthews

Nicholas Allan

RED FOX

'Have a biccy, Dr Matthews.' Kitty opened the first aid box and Matthews dipped his paw in. The lid suddenly shut with a loud snap.

'Aaaargh!' yelped Dr Matthews.

Dr Bickerbeak was standing in front him: he had shut the lid. Dr Bickerbeak was taking Sally's place while she was away.

'Biscuits in the first aid box, Matthews? What a way to run a hospital. What if one of your staff needed a bandage, eh?' said Dr Bickerbeak.

'They'd find them in the biscuit tin, of course,' growled Dr Matthews.

'Not good enough, Matthews. Just not good enough. There's going to be changes around here – a lot of changes.'

The ambulance sped through the snow, arrived at the
hospital, and soon the two Teds were pushing a trolley
down the corridor.

'Ah, Teds, what've you got there?' said Dr Bickerbeak.

'Essential supplies,' said one of the Teds.

'Essential emergency supplies,' said the other Ted.

'Brave of you to drive through the blizzard. Let's see
what you've got.'

Dr Bickerbeak lifted the sheet and party balloons drifted up. 'What's this?' he demanded.

'Essential supplies for Dr Matthews' birthday. Cake ingredients, cheese and onion crisps –'

'Birthday party? There'll be no birthday parties in this hospital while I'm here,' Dr Bickerbeak said, sharply.

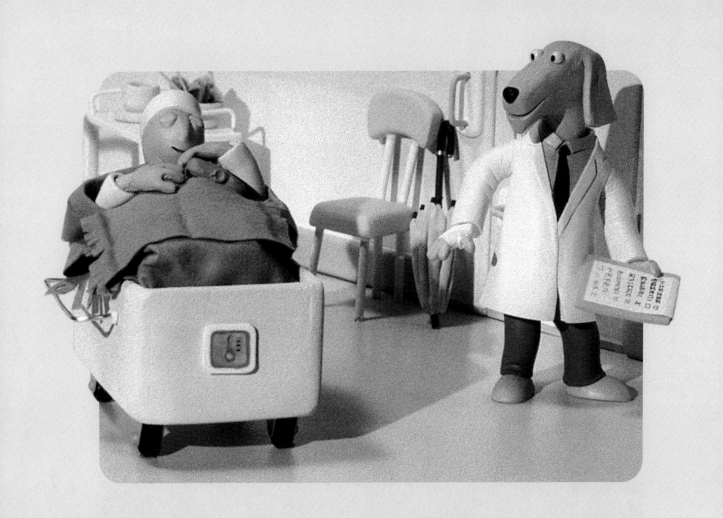

While Dr Matthews was strolling down the corridor,
he noticed Dr Atticus lying in a laundry basket.
'Morning, Atticus.'
'Oh, hello, Matthews. Thought I'd settle in here for
a while. It's a bit chilly in the wards.'

Dr Matthews went to look at the temperature gauge. It was almost at zero, so he went down to the boiler room. There, Dr Bickerbeak was turning off the heating.

'It's too hot in the wards, Dr Matthews. Such a waste of fuel.'

'It *is* winter, Dr Bickerbeak,' growled Dr Matthews. 'The coldest time of year. When birds usually fly away because it's so cold.'

Dr Bickerbeak turned up his beak and stalked out. If this continues, Dr Matthews thought, someone is soon going to get a sore throat.

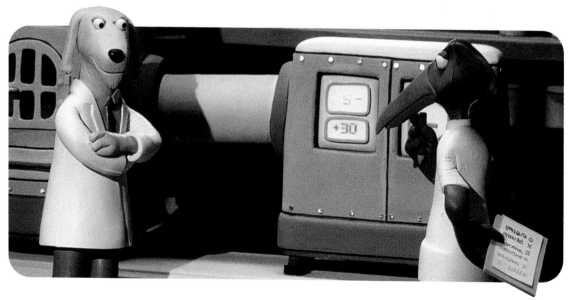

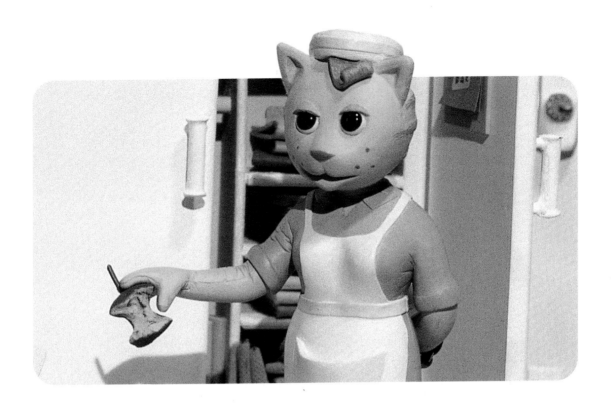

Someone soon did.

But no one could find any cough medicine in the Dispensary. All Kitty found was an old apple core on one of the shelves.

'If you hadn't turned down the heating, Dr Bickerbeak, Geraldine Giraffe wouldn't have a sore throat,' complained Dr Matthews.

'And if you kept your cabinets in order, we might have some cough medicine.'

'It didn't seem important,' said Dr Matthews. 'After all, you don't go to hospital for a sore throat. It's not usually a problem.'

'Not usually, no, Dr Matthews. But for Geraldine it's a very big problem indeed.' And with that, Dr Bickerbeak marched back to the ward.

Dr Matthews sat in the staff room, looking miserable.

'It's all my fault,' he said to Kitty. 'And now we're not going to have a party.'

'At least Clare and Arthur will make your Very Special Birthday Cake, Dr Matthews.'

'Oh yes. I'd forgotten about that. It's lucky the Teds got those essential ingredients for the mixture. Pity they couldn't have got that cough medicine for Geraldine...'

Kitty looked at Dr Matthews. 'Wait a minute! Cough medicine is a mixture, isn't it?'

'Yes.'

'Well, perhaps Clare and Arthur might have the ingredients to mix some up.'

Matthews thought for a moment. 'Kitty, you're an angel,' he said. Then he kissed her.

Clare and Arthur were busy making the Very Special Birthday Cake when Dr Matthews and Nurse Kitty arrived.

'Do you think you could make some cough medicine?' asked Dr Matthews.

'If we stop doing this, your cake will be ruined,' Arthur warned. 'This is the critical moment. We're about to add 200 grammes of thick, scrummy chocolate.'

Dr Matthews didn't want them to stop, especially after tasting the mixture, but Kitty nudged him.

'I'm afraid you'll have to,' he said unhappily. 'The patient must come first.'

No Sally, no birthday party, and now no birthday cake thought Dr Matthews, as he sat in the staff room.

Nurse Kitty tried to cheer him up. She made tea and offered him a biscuit from the first aid box. Dr Matthews bit into one, and pulled a face.

'What's the matter?' asked Kitty.

Dr Matthews pulled out a length of bandage from his mouth.

As night fell, the snow gradually stopped. It was peaceful in the ward; everyone was fast asleep, even Geraldine. That afternoon, Dr Matthews had given her Clare and Arthur's medicine – and it had worked.

Early the next morning Dr Bickerbeak found Nurse Kitty in the Dispensary.

'Where's Dr Matthews?' he snapped. 'He's supposed to be at work by now.'

'Dr Matthews spent all last night tidying the medicine cabinets,' said Kitty.

'Oh,' said Dr Bickerbeak, looking at the tidy shelves around him. 'That was very kind of him.'

'He's a very good doctor really, and a wonderful dog,' said Kitty. 'He was so tired, he slept in the staff room. I'll wake him up.'

'No, no, let sleeping dogs lie, Kitty. Perhaps I have been a bit hard on him. After all, it is his birthday.'

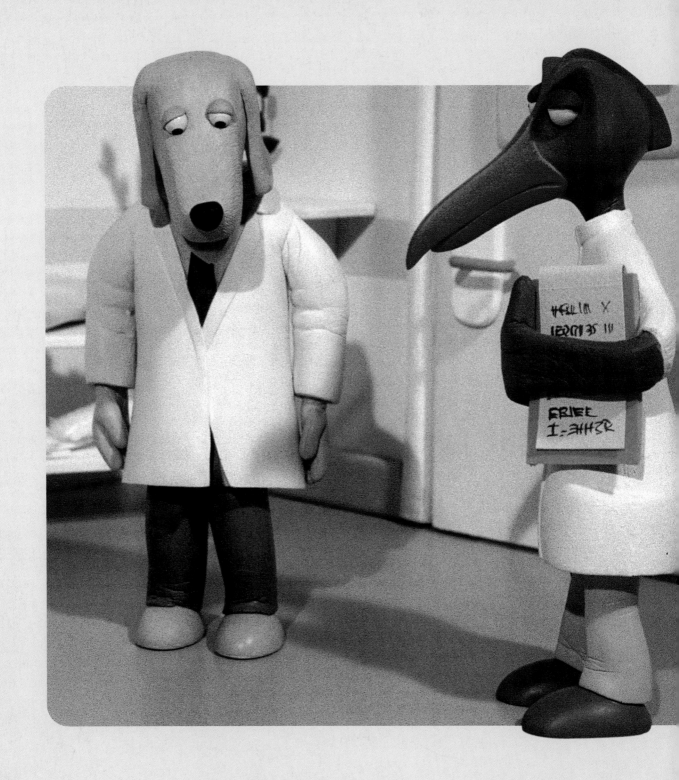

Dr Matthews was having a wonderful dream about Sally, when suddenly he woke up. He looked at his watch, yelped, and hurried to the ward. There, Dr Bickerbeak was also looking at his watch.

'Just in time for lunch, Dr Matthews,' he said. 'It's a good job I was here to make sure everything was in order, wasn't it?'

'Yes, Dr Bickerbeak.'

'Especially to see that everything was prepared... for your birthday.'

Before Dr Matthews could say anything, a bed-screen was pulled back. Behind it were all the staff with party essentials: balloons, cheese and onion crisps – and a huge Very Special Birthday Cake. 'Surprise!' everyone cried. 'But I thought the cake was ruined,' said Dr Matthews.

'We discovered a quick-acting formula,' Clare explained.

'Who's going to try it first?' asked Arthur.

'Me,' said a voice from above. It was Geraldine. So they cut her a slice.

'Delicious!' she said.

As they handed round the cake, a birthday card arrived. *From Sally. Be back on Monday,'* she'd written. It was the best birthday present Dr Matthews could have had.

'Dr Matthews, hurry! There's only one slice of cake left,'
said Kitty.

'But Dr Bickerbeak hasn't had any.'

'You have it, Dr Matthews,' said Dr Bickerbeak.

'No, no, it's yours.'

'No, no, I insist –'

Just then, Geraldine cut the last slice in half.
Dr Matthews and Dr Bickerbeak each took a piece
and tasted it. Both agreed it was the best cake they'd
ever tasted!